| DATE DUE | | |
|---|---|---|
| | | |
| | | |
| | | |
| | | |
| | | |
| | | |
| | | |
| | | |
| | | |
| | | |
| | | |
| | | |

0L00431270

**FIC**  Seidler, Tor.
**SEI**

**Terpin**

# TERPIN

# TOR SEIDLER

❧

# TERPIN

❧

ILLUSTRATIONS BY

## Peter McCarty

LAURA GERINGER BOOKS
*An Imprint of HarperCollinsPublishers*

Terpin

Copyright © 1982 by Tor Seidler

Illustrations copyright © 2002 by Peter McCarty

The text of this work was originally published in 1982 by Farrar, Straus & Giroux.
Printed in the United States of America. For information address
HarperCollins Children's Books, a division of HarperCollins Publishers,
1350 Avenue of the Americas, New York, NY 10019.
www.harpercollins.com

Library of Congress Cataloging-in-Publication Data

Seidler, Tor.

    Terpin / Tor Seidler ; illustrations by Peter McCarty.

        p.    cm.

    Summary: When his well-intentioned lie appears to have contributed to a man's
suicide, Terpin's resolve to never again act or speak, except by the truth in his heart,
has far-reaching consequences.

    ISBN 0-06-623607-X — ISBN 0-06-623608-8 (lib. bdg.)

    [1. Honesty—Fiction. 2. Conduct of life—Fiction. 3. Suicide—Fiction.]

I. McCarty, Peter, ill.  II. Title.

PZ7.S45526 Te  2002                                          2001016685

[Fic]—dc21                                                        CIP

                                                                    AC

Typography by Alicia Mikles

1  2  3  4  5  6  7  8  9  10

❖

First HarperCollins Edition, 2002

*For John Bass*

# 1

"Excuse me, Your Honor, sir, but North Haven is the next stop, 'bout twenty-five minutes."

Awakening, Terpin Taft blinked up at a face with a long white beard. For an instant this gave him a start, for once before in his life, many years ago, he had awakened to see a face with just such a flowing white beard. But he realized it was the conductor.

"North Haven is next, Your Honor," the conductor repeated, touching the brim of his cap. "Or North Tafton, as I hear they're changing it to."

Terpin Taft thanked him. As the old man bowed and shuffled off down the train car, Terpin turned from the ogling eyes of the other passengers and glanced out the window at the hills still mottled with snow. He leaned back and closed his eyes again. Soon he heard passengers whispering.

"Is it really him?" "Of course it is, can't you tell? He was born in North Haven, you know, I read it in the paper." "It's funny somebody so important should be traveling alone, don't you think?" "Well, you know what they say—all great people are lonely deep down. Don't you think there's something lonely about his face?"

In a minute Terpin heard a throat cleared and reopened his eyes, which silenced all the whispering around him. The elderly conductor was standing over him again, cap in hand, a sheepish look on his face.

"Excuse me, Your Honor, sir, but I thought maybe you'd give me your autograph—for my missus. She'd be tickled pink." Terpin took the man's piece of paper, and the conductor murmured, "Lands, this is the most excitement we've had on the line since . . . well, since the tragedy on the North Trestle thirty-odd years ago."

On the piece of paper Terpin wrote: *To my old*

*friend George, who once let me ride without a ticket, and his wife, with best wishes, Terpin Taft.*

"Lands!" the conductor said, reading the inscription. "You mean to say you've ridden this train before, Your Honor? And I let you ride for free?"

Indeed, he had ridden this train before—dozens of times. But that was long before he was "Your Honor," long before there was anything "lonely about his face." Now Terpin was on his way back to his hometown to be honored, now he was a "great man." But why dwell on his greatness? As an ancient Greek philosopher said, Being is nothing, becoming is everything.

Thirty-odd years ago Terpin, who was then a schoolboy with a clean face and slightly moppish brown hair, was riding this same train home to North Haven after a dutiful Thanksgiving visit to his grandmother downstate. It had not been a very entertaining visit. His grandmother was cantankerous and deaf, the turkey had been cooked three hours too long, and the bed in her guest room creaked if he so much as wiggled a toe. But he had said—or rather shouted into his grandmother's hearing aid—that the turkey was delicious, and that morning he'd assured her that he'd slept like a top. For he was, as his schoolmates said, a "good egg."

On this day long ago a man in a black greatcoat boarded the train a few stops before North Haven and sat down beside him. The train had not pulled out of the station before the man heaved a deep sigh. At the fourth or fifth sigh, Terpin had to glance at him. The man was large and had a strong, rugged face, like that of a retired athlete, and for some reason this made the tear running down the man's cheek fill Terpin with compassion.

"Excuse me, sir," Terpin said. "Would you like me to go to the club car and get you a cup of tea?"

The man merely shook his head, so Terpin turned and looked out the window at the hills, which were blanketed with the first snow of the year. But after a minute the man heaved another sigh.

"Is there anything the matter, sir?" Terpin asked.

"Oh, well," the man said, wiping his cheek with the sleeve of his black greatcoat, "it's just my wife."

"Your wife?"

The man nodded.

"I lost her yesterday."

"How did you lose her, sir?"

"In an operation."

"What operation was that?"

The man glanced at him.

"You wouldn't have heard of it, son."

"I might have," said Terpin, who was considered one of the brightest in his class.

"Well," the man sighed, "it was an operation called a hepaticostomy."

After a moment Terpin said: "Oh. It was unsuccessful?"

The man nodded grimly, and another tear rolled down a groove in his rugged cheek.

"Take it from me, boy," he murmured, "life's a rotten business."

This new tear seemed to fall right on Terpin's heart.

"I know it," he agreed with a sigh of his own. "Have you ever heard of Lake Queechee?"

"Sure, up by North Haven."

"My parents were canoeing there one day," Terpin said sadly, "when a storm came up. The canoe went over, and they drowned."

The man turned and stared at him, aghast.

"Both? They both drowned?"

Terpin put on a long face.

"They never found the bodies. In the paper they said it might be on account of the snapping turtles. There're some big ones in the lake, over a hundred years old."

"Snapping turtles!" the man said, growing paler.

By the next stop the man in the black great-coat was no longer sighing. He was far too busy trying to comfort Terpin to worry about himself. As the train neared North Haven, the man brought an old rough-edged coin out of his pocket and handed it to Terpin.

"Here, boy."

"What is it?" Terpin asked.

"Have you ever studied ancient Greece?"

"I just did a paper on Socrates," said Terpin, making up to himself for his ignorance of the operation. "For ancient and medieval history class."

"Well, it's an ancient Greek coin. It's supposed to be good luck." The man shook his head sadly. "I only wish I'd given it to my wife before she went into the hospital."

"Oh, no, it's much too valuable," Terpin said, handing it back.

The man tried again to give him the ancient coin, but Terpin had been brought up well enough to know not to accept such a gift from a stranger. And as the train pulled into North Haven, he slipped out past the man and shook his hand good-bye.

On the platform he quickly caught sight of his best friend, Charles Ackley, a tall, gangly boy whose head loomed above all the others. Charles was holding a football tucked under his arm exactly as the legendary "Raw" Runyan, in the bronze statue in the display case at their high school, held the bronze football under his.

"Hiya, Taft," Charles said, smacking him on the back. "Let's get a move on."

Terpin glanced a little longingly at the snowy hills, where he would have liked to go cross-country skiing. But the football season was not quite over, and although the day after Thanksgiving was a school holiday, they still had football practice, for the South Haven game was next week.

"I've got to drop this off at home," Terpin said, indicating his suitcase.

The way to his house led them through the middle of North Haven. North Haven was a lovely town, small and quaint and sleepy—so sleepy that even the Union soldier on the town green, who was made of bronze, looked as if he would have fallen asleep on his granite pedestal had his long rifle not held him up. After crossing the green, they walked out a road called the Pepper Pike, so named because it ran through a dreamlike birch wood: the little black spots on the white bark looked like pepper. Since Terpin was carrying his suitcase, Charles had to toss the football with himself. Soon the ball was covered with slush, for Charles had very long feet, which he was forever tripping over.

"You practice the piano yesterday?" Terpin asked.

Like his feet, Charles's fingers were long—long and supple.

"Nah," Charles said. "I keep telling you, not during the season."

Soon they came to a large white clapboard house with green shutters. Charles waited on the front porch, practicing hand-offs to an invisible running back, while Terpin wiped his feet on the mat and slipped in the door. He tried to set his suitcase quietly by the umbrella stand, but as he turned to slip back out, the dog bounded up to him with a joyful bark.

"Terpin, is that you?" came a sweet voice from the card room.

He had no choice but to show his face in the card room and undergo an examination about

Thanksgiving with his grandmother. Sitting at the table with the green felt top, as on nearly every afternoon of the year, were Mrs. Beale, a plump lady who lived next door; Terpin's Aunt Nettles, who was anything but plump and looking very grim; and his Uncle Guy, who was stirring the ice around in his scotch with a finger. The fourth in this game of canasta was Terpin's mother: for the drowning story Terpin had told on the train was not strictly true, had only been intended to cheer up the man in the black greatcoat. Terpin's father, director of the North Haven Savings and Loan, was also very much alive and had not set foot in a canoe in his life.

"Hey, Terp, old boy, how was the turkey down there?" Uncle Guy asked. "Pretty stringy, I bet."

Uncle Guy and Aunt Nettles lived in the house with them because Uncle Guy was his mother's brother. Aunt Nettles did not care for this situation any more than Terpin's father did; but Uncle Guy usually managed to stay in good spirits. The four cardplayers had hardly missed an afternoon of canasta in Terpin's memory, and for the last seven or eight years they had kept a running score on a thick yellow pad by Aunt Nettles's elbow.

"It was all right," Terpin said of the turkey. "How's the game?"

"Well, if your Aunt Nettles dropped dead tomorrow," Uncle Guy said, repeating a wish he often expressed, "it'd still take them two years to catch up, and your poor old uncle three."

"Poor is right," Aunt Nettles muttered, looking up from her cards.

"Oh, do drop dead, dear," Uncle Guy said brightly, moving the ice in his glass with his stirring finger.

"Terpin, lamb, why don't you go and unpack your suitcase?" Mrs. Taft suggested.

"I've got to go to football practice, Mom. Charles is waiting."

"Oh, well, don't be late for dinner," she said, football practice being something of which her husband approved.

"Good-bye Mrs. Beale, good-bye Aunt Nettles, good-bye Uncle Guy, good-bye Mom," Terpin said politely.

And as he went into the front hall, he could not help smiling as he heard Mrs. Beale say, "Really, he's such a nice boy, such a little gentleman."

It often seemed to Terpin that the locker room in the school gymnasium contained more mud than the practice field outside, but the smell, which he hated, resulted less from the mud than from the damp sweaty clothes piled in the foot of the lockers. Once he and Charles had changed into their clammy gear, they jogged out onto the half-frozen field, where the coach was blowing his whistle to line the team up for calisthenics. As Terpin took his place for jumping jacks, helmeted heads turned and said, "Hey, Terp," "Hiya, Terp." After jumping jacks came a neck exercise in which half of them got down on all fours like dogs while the others put all their weight on the backs of their helmets. During this ordeal Terpin found it especially hard not to wish he was gliding silently through the woods on his cross-country skis. But later, during passing drill, he made a diving catch in the mud, and the coach, whom they secretly called The Chin, came over and clapped him on the back.

"Good catch, Taft," said the coach, whose jutting chin was level with the top of Terpin's helmet. "Didn't hurt so much, did it?"

Terpin's left elbow was bleeding, and his hands were numb. "Nah," he replied.

"That's what I like to hear," the coach said, smacking him again. "Listen, you lunkheads, if you all played as hard as Taft here, we'd take South Haven by three touchdowns."

The finest moment of football practice came, however, when it was over, when they all trooped out of the smelly locker room to go home. A circle of girls, deep in conversation, stood under the leafless elm in the schoolyard, even today, a holiday. Like two blobs seen under a microscope in biology class, the two groups came together, then split up into a number of smaller blobs. Terpin ended up, as always, with Melanie Minor, who had the longest, shiniest hair in school, the color of a harvest moon, reddish gold. Melanie Minor was "all-round." She was captain of the girls' field hockey team, she got straight A's, and she had a wonderful way of smiling with her green eyes. Today, however, her green eyes had a troubled look, which was every bit as pretty. She was worried about the Punic Wars. On Monday she was going to have to deliver a paper on this subject to their ancient and medieval history class, and since Terpin had gotten so much applause for his recent paper on Socrates, she wanted him to read hers over and see if he thought it would do.

They went into the soda parlor near the Town Building. Her paper was not long, and Terpin finished it before their "Green Rivers" had come. A Green River was a sweet, syrupy beverage which he did not particularly like but which Melanie insisted on, since it was all the rage. He did not like her account of the Punic Wars any better, finding it dull and lifeless, perhaps even copied from an encyclopedia.

"Well?" Melanie asked, when he had flipped over the last page.

"What are you worried about? Thrushy always gives you A's."

Thrushy was their name for Mr. Thrushcroft, the history teacher, who did, in fact, have many birdlike characteristics.

"But do you like it?" asked Melanie, who sometimes worried that she got A's partly because her mother was North Haven's mayor.

"That's really something," Terpin said brightly, "how the Romans ground salt into their fields so nothing would grow."

But at this Melanie screwed her face into a pout and began to flatten her straw on the table.

"You don't like it," she said tragically.

"Of course I like it!"

"No, you don't."

"Sure I do."

"Really? Cross your heart?"

"Cross my heart," Terpin said.

Her face slowly brightened, and she gave him a smile, shrugging her long shiny hair back behind her shoulders.

"Well, if you know what's good for you, you better lead the cheering section on Monday," she said with mock severity.

"Will a standing ovation do?"

She reached over and touched his sleeve.

"Terpin, there's a bloodstain."

"Oh, I just scraped my elbow in practice."

"But it's still bleeding! Does it hurt?"

It had stung sharply in the shower and still did a little; but he said it was nothing.

"Roll up your sleeve," she ordered.

It was very pleasant to have Melanie dip the corner of her napkin into her water and dab it ever so gently on his bloody elbow. A few minutes later he walked her home to the mayor's mansion, situated at the other end of the town green, and it was pleasanter still that she should leave off her deerskin gloves and let him hold her hand.

"Thank you for liking my paper, Terpin," she said, giving his hand a squeeze as she went in at her gate.

He remained on the icy sidewalk outside the picket fence, and as she opened the front door, she turned and gave him a last little wave, which warmed him in spite of the freezing wind.

Turning away, he walked with a springy step toward a white pillared building nearby. The building looked rather like one of the Greek temples they had been studying in history but was really the North Haven Savings and Loan. It was not a business holiday, and his father was just getting ready to leave the office when he came in. His father was a portly, well-respected man who always wore a pocket watch with a gold chain that hung across his vest. When he was displeased, his face turned quite red, starting, oddly enough, at his forehead and working down gradually past his nose and cheeks to his chin. But when pleased, he smiled and pushed back his suit coat to insert two fingers in his vest pocket, and this was what he did today when Terpin came into his office.

"Home again," Mr. Taft said, leaning back in his chair. "You make practice?"

Terpin nodded, and Mr. Taft smiled.

"I ran into that Mr. Thrushcroft at lunch today," Mr. Taft went on. "Queer bird, isn't he? But he tells me you did a bang-up job on your history paper."

Knowing Mr. Thrushcroft's elaborate and old-fashioned way of speaking, Terpin sincerely doubted he had said "bang-up job"; but still he smiled. Mr. Taft shook his head with a sigh, admitting it had been an awfully long time since he had been in school.

"On Socrates, he told me. He was the one who did himself in, right?"

"He drank a cup of poison hemlock," Terpin replied, "because he wouldn't lie to the court. He said your life should express what you truly believe."

"Good for him," Mr. Taft said, nodding approvingly. "And speaking of believing in things, what do you think of this, son? In twenty years, when you'll be sitting behind this desk, this town'll be on the map."

The "this" Mr. Taft was referring to was a scale model, set out on his desktop, of a development of summer cabins and ski chalets to be built on one side of the Pepper Pike. This had been Mr. Taft's pet scheme for some years, and with the help of Melanie's mother he had recently gotten the approval of the town council. The bank was financing the ambitious project, hoping to transform sleepy North Haven into a thriving tourist town, to which people would be drawn in the summer by nearby Lake Queechee and in the winter by the skiing. Mr. Taft continued to talk about Heavenly Havens, as the development was to be called, as they walked home together along the Pepper Pike. But the twilight had turned the snow and the birches a soft lilac color, and in spite of the rosy future his father was painting, Terpin could not help feeling sad at the prospect of the dreamlike white trees being chopped down.

"It'll be the best thing ever happened to this whistle-stop," Mr. Taft said, "won't it?"

"I guess so, Dad."

"Course you'll get more out of it than the old guard, like me. By the time you take over the reins, the money'll be coming in hand over fist. Then you can expand. Right?"

"Sure, Dad, I guess so."

"*Guess* so!"

"Sure, Dad, we'll expand."

Mr. Taft tousled Terpin's moppish hair good-naturedly. "That's the spirit, son."

As they neared the little general store at the end of the Pepper Pike, Terpin decided he ought to take advantage of his father's good mood, which he knew would be strained as soon as he got home and saw Uncle Guy drinking his good scotch.

"May I have a quarter for a cake of ski wax, Dad?" he asked.

"Gonna break out the old boards this weekend?" Mr. Taft said, digging in a pocket. "Here you go. I'll see you at home."

The little store was run by the local "crazy," as Nora Strout was known at school. She was a square, balding woman in a dirty smock. The story went that as a girl, working for her father, poor Nora had found that the only way she could get any attention, being so homely, was to be slow in serving people. Now that she ran the store herself, she never waited on you unless you paid her a compliment. After pointing out a cake of blue wax in the glass counter at the back of the place, Terpin looked up at the ugly woman, who was waiting grimly behind the counter with her meaty arms crossed. He complimented her cheeks.

"They have such a nice blush today, Nora," he said. "They remind me of those Crimson Glory roses my mother won the flower show with."

Nora's grim expression melted into a toothy smile, and while her cheeks were not much like roses, her yellow teeth were rather like a sunflower—with several petals missing. She opened the case and brought out the cake of wax. But as he walked the rest of the way home, Terpin saw he would not be able to ski until the morning, for darkness had gathered over the snowy hills.

For dinner there was a ham, which brought on Uncle Guy's usual stories about the acting days of his carefree youth, when he had been on casual terms with any number of hams. After taking her seat, Aunt Nettles looked up peevishly at the bright chandelier over the dining-room table, which Mr. Taft had turned on to carve by. Shading her eyes, she announced that brain surgery could be done on the table.

"Any time you feel, Nettie," Mr. Taft said wearily, "that you should assume the carving duties in this household, you're welcome to lop off your fingers by candlelight."

"Did you have a long hard day, dear?" Mrs. Taft asked soothingly.

"Yes, I'm afraid I did," Mr. Taft sighed. "A lot of brainwork."

Aunt Nettles gave a little snort. After winking at Terpin, Uncle Guy said:

"I'm sorry, dearest, did you say something?"

Aunt Nettles shot her husband a withering look. "You know very well I didn't."

"Oh," Uncle Guy said, nodding. "Then it must have just been a snort of sarcasm."

Serving himself last, Mr. Taft took his seat at the head of the table.

"Sarcasm?" he said, wrinkling his brow. "Who's being sarcastic?"

"Eat up, everyone," said Mrs. Taft.

"It's only Nettles," said Uncle Guy. "She snorted sarcastically while you were describing your brainwork."

Mr. Taft sat back in his chair and turned to Aunt Nettles. "Is that so?" he asked, a look of surprise spreading slowly over his face.

"Of course not," Aunt Nettles muttered.

"Bite your tongue!" cried Uncle Guy.

"Shush!" cried Aunt Nettles.

"Please!" cried Mrs. Taft.

"But she did!" cried Uncle Guy.

"I did not!" cried Aunt Nettles. "Did I, Terpin?"

"Don't ask me," Terpin said with a shrug.

"Did you have a nice ride on the train, lamb?" Mrs. Taft asked, changing the subject.

Terpin nodded.

"Lucky you didn't miss your stop," Mr. Taft said. "I heard a late bulletin on the radio about how a man jumped off the train up at the North Trestle. They had an hour delay while they dragged the corpse up out of the gorge. Quite a tragedy."

"I'll bet ten dollars his wife drove him to it," Uncle Guy said.

"I can think of a few ne'er-do-wells who ought to be ashamed they *haven't* jumped off a bridge," Aunt Nettles muttered.

"He left a suicide note pinned to his seat, poor devil," Mr. Taft went on. "Something about how life's a rotten business. Now, in my book, business is going to get better and better."

Terpin looked up from his peas. It seemed to him he had heard that sentiment about life somewhere else recently. So after dinner, while helping his mother dry the dishes, he turned on the radio. When the news came on, the announcer described how the man had leapt to his death off the trestle bridge.

"The deceased, who was wearing a black greatcoat, is still unidentified," the announcer said. "As for his reasons, all we have to go by so far is the note he left behind pinned to his seat: 'Life's a rotten business where men lose their wives and children lose their parents.'"

At these words the good china platter fell out of Terpin's hands. It shattered into a hundred pieces on the floor.

# 2

Terpin could not get any of his weekend homework out of the way that evening, for his mind was stuck on the man in the black greatcoat. He wandered into the living room and sat down with the rest of the family in front of the fire, but he heard not a word that was said to him, merely shaking or nodding his dazed head as he stared into the hearth. He felt that something inside him had suddenly turned from white to black, like the birch logs in the fire. The story he had told the man in the black greatcoat, meant to cheer him up, had ended up contributing to the man's depression, perhaps even pushing him over the brink.

At nine-thirty he trudged upstairs. His cross-country skis were leaning in the corner of his room, but he did not wax them for the morning, as he had intended to do. He merely emptied the few pennies from his pants pocket onto his desk, which was littered with the library books he had taken out for his paper on Socrates, and got undressed.

But he could not sleep. He lay staring into the darkness, a darkness that seemed a reflection of his soul, and he asked himself over and over why he had told that lie on the train. But of course it was too late now for regrets to do any good.

Every time a twig snapped outdoors in the cold, he felt it was happening somewhere inside him. Between snaps, he heard his parents and Aunt Nettles climb the stairs to bed; and he was still awake when Uncle Guy, who always outlasted Mr. Taft's vigilance over the liquor cabinet, passed by his door, the ice tinkling in his glass. After the creaky bed at his grandmother's last night, the train ride, and football practice, Terpin was exhausted. But in his mind he kept seeing the black greatcoat flapping around the poor man as he fell from the bridge into the gorge.

Finally he tried to put this black image out of his mind by thinking of the white snow he would slice with his skis in the morning. In the end he decided to get up and wax his skis after all, in the hope that this would distract his brain. He turned on a lamp and padded over to his winter coat, draped over his desk chair; but as he reached for the cake of wax in the pocket, he touched something else. A shiver went through him as his fingers closed on a cold, rough-edged little disk. He pulled it out. It was the ancient Greek coin he had refused on the train. Somehow, when he got up to get off, the man had managed to slip it into his pocket, that man who was now dead.

His hand began to shake, and the coin dropped onto the desk. He looked at it. On one side there was an owl. He flipped it over gingerly, as if it were scalding hot. Dimly engraved on the other side was a seated man, and unlikely as it seemed, the homely bearded face of the man resembled the sculpted face of Socrates illustrated on the cover of one of the library books. This made him even more uneasy, and he put the coin away in his strongbox. Why did the man have to give him this keepsake, as if the mere memory of him were not haunting enough? Good luck indeed!—he had already broken his mother's favorite platter. He turned off the light, dismissing the ski-waxing idea entirely, and crawled back into the warmth of the bed. Again he wondered why he had had to tell the man the lie about his parents. Why? . . . Why? . . . Why? . . . The question beat against his brain, over and over and over, until finally, like the sound of waves breaking on a shore, it lulled him to sleep. . . .

"Wake up, Terpin."

He opened his eyes. It was dawn; a gentle golden light showed in the window. A robed figure with a long flowing white beard was standing over his bed. The man looked very wise, so Terpin asked:

"Why did I have to tell the man that lie?"

"What did you learn from your history paper?" the man replied, answering his question with a question.

"That your life should express what you truly believe," he murmured.

"Did you truly believe your parents were drowned in the lake?"

Terpin shook his head on the pillow. Suddenly he realized that the man standing over him was the ancient Greek philosopher himself, Socrates.

"Are you ever going to lie again?" Socrates asked.

Terpin shook his head. Socrates handed him the ancient Greek coin.

"You will never speak or act except by the truth in your heart."

"I will never speak or act except by the truth in my heart," Terpin said, clenching the coin fervently in his hand.

"Your life will be an expression of what you truly believe."

"My life will be an expression of what I truly believe."

"Good-bye," Socrates said. "Sleep well."

"Good-bye, sleep well," Terpin murmured, his lids closing heavily.

When he woke again, it was nearly noon. His first emotion on seeing the clock was disappointment: he had slept so long that he would not have time to ski before football practice. Then he remembered the horror of the man in the black greatcoat and the wonder of the dream he had had of the man with the white beard. Feeling something in his hand, he opened his fist. There was the ancient Greek coin he had put away in his strongbox.

## 3

Mr. Thrushcroft was the sort of teacher to inspire jokes among his pupils. The history teacher had a dainty, birdlike figure with skinny arms and legs and a plump little belly. Instead of sitting behind his broad desk he often perched on the front of it, rocking gently to and fro, as if in a breeze. And when he addressed the class, he used ornate and old-fashioned language. But in spite of all this his students made few jokes about him, except to call him "Thrushy" off school grounds, for his eloquent tongue could also be very sharp.

Ancient and medieval history was Terpin's last class of the day. It was also the only class he had with his friend Charles Ackley, and when Terpin came into the classroom on Monday and took his alphabetically assigned seat in the back row, Charles swiveled around in his desk in the front row and made a series of faces and signals, which seemed aimed at expressing surprise at seeing him in school. But this dumb show ended abruptly when Mr. Thrushcroft looked up from his grade book, where he had been making an entry, and brought the class to order. Mr. Thrushcroft rose on his spindly legs and came around the front of the desk, a paper dangling limply in his hand.

"Last Wednesday we were the privileged audience for Mr. Taft's address on Socrates," the teacher said. "In the interim I have had the opportunity to look over the essay at leisure."

As Terpin was well aware, the fact that the class had been a "privileged audience" meant nothing at all, this being merely one of Mr. Thrushcroft's flowery ways of putting things. But then the teacher went on:

"As you know, I'm not in the habit of casting pearls before swine"—this clearly mystified half the class—"but Mr. Taft is perhaps as far from a swine as any student I've had in the last few years. This paper is Haversham quality."

Being "far from a swine" was quite a compliment; but that the paper was "Haversham quality" created a genuine stir. The Haversham Award was given each winter to the student who wrote the best essay on a topic in history chosen by the principal of the school. In the glass display case out in the hall, next to the bronze statue of the legendary "Raw" Runyan running the football, was a plaque commemorating the Haversham Award winners over the last fifty years.

Mr. Thrushcroft handed the paper to someone in the front row, and it was duly passed back to Terpin. The teacher then perched on the front of the desk.

"And today we have what I'm sure will be the inestimable pleasure of hearing Miss Minor's account of the Punic Wars."

Blushing prettily, Melanie rose from her seat in the middle of the room and went up to the blackboard. Once she had arranged her hair behind her shoulders, she began to read her paper.

"The Punic Wars were a series of three horrible wars fought between Rome and Carthage to see who would control the Mediterranean Sea. The First Punic War started in 264 B.C. and ended in 241 B.C. The Second Punic War started in 218 B.C. and ended in 201 B.C., six years shorter than the First Punic War. The Third Punic War started in 149 B.C. and ended in 146 B.C., fourteen years shorter than the Second Punic War. Even though it was the longest of the Punic Wars, the First Punic War was not as famous as the Second Punic War. . . ."

Ten minutes later it was finally over, and most of the class clapped as Melanie made her way back to her seat, bringing another pretty blush to her cheeks. For the last half of her paper, Mr. Thrushcroft had rocked happily to and fro on the front of the desk; and he stopped only when the applause ended.

"Thank you very much indeed, Miss Minor, for a thought-provoking and well-delivered essay," he said. "Any comments, class? Yes, Mr. Schwartz?"

"I liked the part about Hannibal and the elephants, sir."

"I see you were listening, Mr. Schwartz. Miss Capelli?"

"I thought it was very well delivered, Mr. Thrushcroft."

"We're of one mind there, Miss Capelli. I only wish her mother had been present to hear it." He looked around, but no other hands were raised. "Mr. Taft, I'm sure we'd welcome your expert opinion."

Terpin, who had been staring at some inky, time-worn initials carved on his desk, blinked up at the sound of his name.

"Excuse me, sir?"

"Your appraisal of Miss Minor's essay," Mr. Thrushcroft said benignly.

Glancing over her shoulder, Melanie shot Terpin the briefest of glances, her green eyes smiling through the curtain of her harvest-moon hair. But Terpin remained silent, merely staring at the title of his own paper lying on his desk.

"Come, Mr. Taft, surely you have some overall

impression for our enlightenment."

Terpin sighed.

"Well, overall, sir," he murmured, "I guess I found it a little . . . tiresome."

This pronouncement had a more sensational effect than Mr. Thrushcroft's mention of the Haversham Award. The class gasped as one. Melanie again glanced over her shoulder, but this time her eyes were not smiling, and the benign look fell from Mr. Thrushcroft's face. Terpin himself was rather startled at his words.

"Tiresome, did you say, Mr. Taft?"

Terpin opened his mouth to correct himself. But there floated before his eyes a strange image of black and white, of the man in the black greatcoat and the other man with the flowing white beard. And he merely nodded.

"I see," Mr. Thrushcroft said, tapping his beaklike nose. "I hope my little comments on your paper didn't go to your head, Mr. Taft."

"I don't think so, sir."

Mr. Thrushcroft frowned at him. But after a minute he quit his perch on the front of his desk and went to the blackboard, where he began the day's lecture.

After this last class of the day there was the usual stampede to the cloakroom. Terpin tried to make his way to Melanie there, wanting to apologize to her, but her girlfriends had surrounded her like a Swiss guard. And when he called her name, his heart sank further, for all these other girls gave him indignant looks, but Melanie herself did not even glance his way, seeming to be wrapped up in the process of flipping her beautiful hair outside the fur collar of her coat.

Terpin put on his own coat and scarf and trudged sadly out into the hallway. In front of the display case holding the statue of "Raw" Runyan and the Haversham plaque, Charles Ackley came up and gripped his arm.

"Hey, you have a fight with Melanie or something?" he asked.

Terpin shrugged, looking into his friend's face.

"I figured you weren't in school today," Charles went on. "I figured you had the flu."

"The flu?"

"Well, you missed practice all weekend. Coach said you must have the flu."

"Nope, I'm okay."

"Then where were you?"

By now they were outside on the back steps, and Terpin pointed off at the white hills in the distance.

"I was cross-country skiing. It was beautiful, but I got the wrong wax. Too sticky."

"Skiing! Man, what are you talking about? Coach is going to eat you for dinner!"

Terpin shrugged again.

"Want to come with me today, Charles? We can get some red wax."

"Today! But we've got practice! Listen. I'll just tell coach you had the flu."

Charles started to pull him in the direction of the smelly locker rooms, but Terpin stopped at the edge of the first playing field.

"What's the matter, Taft? We've got to hoof it. There's a scrimmage today."

"I'm going skiing."

Charles stared at him, stupefied, and muttered something about The Chin.

"The thing is," Terpin explained, "I don't really like football."

Now Charles looked at him as if he were talking a foreign language. In the distance the coach walked out of the gym onto the frozen field.

"Well, I've got to shake a leg," Charles muttered, finally releasing his arm.

"No, you don't. Why don't you come skiing with me? Or better still, why don't you go home and practice the piano?"

"Why should I practice the piano during the season?"

Terpin sighed. "Because you're better at the piano than football. You play beautifully, Charles."

At this, Charles only frowned. "You saying I'm no good at football?"

It was Terpin's turn to take his friend's arm.

"If you were good at football, Charles, why would you be third string? You've got real talent for the piano, though. But if you never practice, you'll—"

Charles yanked himself free.

"Some friend you turned out to be!" He scowled. "You can go jump in Lake Queechee for all I care—and I hope it ices over on you."

Charles marched across the slushy field toward the gym. Halfway across he tripped over his long feet and fell onto his hands, but when he got up, he still didn't look back, merely slapped his hands angrily against each other. As Terpin turned sadly away, the coach called out from the distance:

"Hey, Taft, you sick?"

As the hulking coach approached him, Terpin wished he *were* sick—wished he had never come to school that day at all. He dug his hands in his pockets, and his left hand closed around the ancient Greek coin. Soon the jutting chin was hovering over him.

"How ya doin', buddy? Feeling better today?"

Terpin shook his head. "I'm feeling worse today, coach."

"Then how come you're not home in bed?"

"Oh, I'm not sick."

The coach squinted down at him, then

clapped him on the back, pushing him toward the gym.

"Better suit up. We don't got all day."

Terpin turned to face the coach. "I don't really like smashing into other people," he said. "I'm going skiing in the woods."

He left the coach standing there with his large jaw hanging open—for, muscular as he was, the coach was slower on the draw than birdlike Mr. Thrushcroft and therefore less intimidating. When Terpin had rounded the school building, he headed across the green for the bank, where he hoped to borrow a quarter from his father for a cake of the red ski wax. But his father was not in his office.

"He's out at the site with the chamber of commerce," said his father's secretary.

"The site" referred to Heavenly Havens; so Terpin walked out the Pepper Pike toward home. His father and several other gentlemen in overcoats and boots were gathered at the edge of the birch wood. As Terpin trudged up to them through the snow, everyone smiled and said,

"Why, here's young Taft." But Mr. Taft himself wore a look of surprise.

"What is it, son?"

"I bought the blue wax, but I should have gotten the red," Terpin explained. "The blue's too sticky."

Mr. Taft unbuttoned his overcoat and pulled out his pocket watch.

"Shouldn't you be at practice?"

"I'm going skiing."

Mr. Taft frowned.

"But you have the South Haven game on Friday."

Terpin shrugged and repeated his true opinion of football. Mr. Taft's face began to redden, starting just under the brim of his fedora hat, and Terpin, who had fifteen cents in his pocket, realized he would probably have to make do with half a cake of wax.

"You run along back to practice, son," Mr. Taft advised. "We have business to discuss."

As Terpin started to traipse away, one of the gentlemen took a cigar out of his mouth and said,

"Where would you start, boy?"

"Start, sir?" Terpin replied.

"We've got to clear from here to the back forty," the man explained. "We thought we'd put up a marker where we cut down the first tree, for posterity."

Terpin, wishing he had escaped, stared around at the lovely birches.

"How's this one strike you?" the man said, pointing his cigar at one of the thicker trunks. "What do you say we let the boy here land the first blow? After all, it's these youngsters who'll reap the fruits."

Terpin began to back away, but the men only smiled, and one of them put an ax in Terpin's hands.

"Give it one to remember you by, right here under the knot," a man said, leading him to the chosen tree.

The rest of the chamber of commerce gathered around. But Terpin dropped the ax in the snow.

"What's wrong, boy?" asked the cigar smoker.

Poor Terpin. It seemed to him that the coin in

his pocket had brought him the worst luck of his life, and he wished more than ever that he had spent the day sick in bed. Now all the chamber of commerce was egging him on to pick up the ax.

"But I can't," Terpin pleaded.

"Why not?"

"Because it would be wrong to cut down the birches."

"Wrong? How could it be wrong?"

"Because it would ruin the town."

The men laughed.

"Hardly, young man," the cigar smoker said with a smile. "In fact, it'll put the town on the map. Someday you'll thank us for it."

"No, I won't," Terpin murmured.

"Don't talk back," said Mr. Taft, who was now red down to his collar. "I'll see you at dinner, Terpin."

Perhaps because his father was simply glad to see the last of him, no comment was made on the fact that Terpin did not head back in the direction of school. At the end of the Pepper Pike he went into the general store for his half cake of wax.

Crazy Nora was standing behind the back counter as usual, her meaty arms crossed.

"May I have half a cake of the red wax please, Nora?" Terpin asked.

She did not move a muscle, except to lift a hand to scratch at the balding place on her head. Terpin sighed and examined her from head to foot. His eyes finally settled on her thick, veiny legs.

"I see you're not wearing stockings, Nora," he said.

For a moment Nora continued to glare at him, but then her expression softened.

"Yup." She grinned, showing her sparse yellow teeth, and opened the glass case. "Some look a fright without stockings, but some can get by."

Terpin paid for the wax and walked home. It was a relief to learn that telling the truth did not always lead to disaster. But to be on the safe side, he avoided another encounter by sneaking in the back door of his house and changing into his ski clothes without alerting the canasta players to his presence. He let the dog in as he went out, and soon he was gliding like a ghost up the wooded hill behind the house. He skied silently. When he was well into the woods, he caught sight of what looked like a small drift of snow blown up against a tree trunk—except that the drift was nibbling the bark. It quit nibbling. Its nose quivered, then off it bounded, leaving behind prints like miniature snowshoes. Of course, Terpin could not match the hare's pace through the trees. But it was exhilarating to try. The rest of the world fell away. There were only the trees, the snow, and the snowshoe hares to make his heart leap.

As he neared the top of the ridge, the bare maples and birches gave way to hemlocks and blue spruces, which perfumed the air with a scent very different from that of the locker room in the gym. At the summit he stopped to catch his breath. All he could hear was his own breathing; the surrounding silence was the furthest thing possible from the shouts and whistles of the coach. The tips of his slender skis stuck out in the air over a cornice. The hillside below was treeless. It was perfectly clean and white and smooth, except for the snaking tracks he had made on it over the weekend. With those curling tracks the secret slope looked, he noticed now for the first time, like Socrates's flowing white beard. His heart gave a new leap. He no longer felt dark inside, as he had the other night; his heart felt as clean and alive as one of the snowshoe hares. How strange that after such an awful day he should suddenly be happier than ever before in his life!

# 4

But others did not seem to be happy with him. The next day in school, when he sat down next to Melanie at lunch, she picked up her tray and moved to another table. From then on, whenever he ran into her in the halls or on the sidewalks, she seemed to look right through him, which made him feel strange and ghostlike, as if he no longer existed. Charles Ackley at least remained on speaking terms with him, in spite of his comments on his friend's football ability, but Terpin soon heard that the coach had called him a "pansy" for preferring the hills to the football field. On Friday afternoon the team managed to beat South Haven without him, however, so he did not have to feel guilty about letting them down. But his father had taken off early from the bank to watch the game, and that night at dinner Mr. Taft was very red in the face.

"What is it, dear?" Mrs. Taft asked gently when they had sat down to the pot roast. "There wasn't a robbery, was there?"

The North Haven Savings and Loan had not been robbed in its two-hundred-year history, but Mrs. Taft often asked this question, knowing that whatever was wrong with her husband could not be as dire as this.

"Why weren't you suited up today?" Mr. Taft asked, frowning at Terpin.

"I was skiing, Dad," Terpin said. "It was beautiful up on the ridge. I saw an owl."

"What was that?" Mr. Taft snapped.

"An owl. A snowy owl, sitting on a stump."

Mr. Taft's face was now anything but snowy.

"You missed the big game for an owl?"

"Nothing wrong with that," Uncle Guy said merrily. "I used to be a night owl myself, before I got hitched. Best days of my life."

"I'm glad to hear you were something, once upon a time," Aunt Nettles muttered. "Now you can't even play canasta."

"Caught her cheating on the score again, Terp, old boy," Uncle Guy confided. "Says she's up three thousand points, when the fact is—"

"The fact is, you couldn't count to ten without slurring the numbers," Aunt Nettles said shrilly.

"Please," Mrs. Taft pleaded, and then she turned to her husband. "I did the potatoes just the way you like them, didn't I, dear?"

"I never thought a son of mine would quit the football team," Mr. Taft said bitterly. "I never felt so ashamed in all my life. Owls! People shouldn't be allowed to quit the team. If you were in a military academy, you couldn't get away with it."

"How can you talk about military academies?" Mrs. Taft said, a little alarmed. "Terpin's a good boy."

"Well, I always thought so," Mr. Taft grumbled, spearing one of the nicely roasted potatoes with his fork. "But telling the chamber of commerce not to cut trees, and now quitting the team right before the big game . . ."

Weeks passed, and little more was said about military academies. By calling Melanie's paper "tiresome," Terpin had alienated most of the girls in his class, and by quitting the football team, he had alienated most of the boys. Somehow, he was no longer a good egg. He was now more of a bad penny, and hardly anyone said, "Hiya, Terp," anymore, except occasionally Charles Ackley. Terpin stopped raising his hand in class and no longer tried to sit with Melanie or members of the football team at lunch, thereby avoiding catastrophes. On the way home from school he made a point of detouring the Pepper Pike, where members of the chamber of commerce often turned up, and around his father he kept his opinions of the Heavenly Havens project to himself. Over Christmas vacation terrible arguments erupted between his aunt and uncle over the seven-years-running canasta score, but during the day Terpin avoided being dragged into their dispute by spending most of his time skiing after snowshoe hares in the woods. He could not, however, escape their haggling in the evenings. In years past, most of his evenings over Christmas vacation had been occupied with yuletide parties given by various classmates; but this year he was not invited. The only party he was asked to was at the Ackleys'. After dinner Charles played carols on the piano, played them beautifully in spite of his lack of practice, and Terpin tried to make up to his friend for his assessment of his football ability by paying him heartfelt compliments on his playing. But the following evening, when the rest of his "friends" had been invited to Melanie's party at the mayor's mansion, he had to sit home again.

After the afternoon card session, Aunt Nettles always took the yellow score sheet and locked it in her jewelry box; but this evening Uncle Guy, who had had a lot of eggnog, found the key to this jewelry box and brought the thick score pad into the living room, where the family was gathered around the fire.

"Here we are, ladies and gents!" Uncle Guy said, waving the pad triumphantly over his head. "Now we can check the figures once and for all."

Mr. Taft did not have enough interest in the

matter to glance up from his financial journal, but Mrs. Taft sighed sadly, and Aunt Nettles looked daggers at her husband.

"Thief," she said.

"Well, there's an old saying I remember from my vaudeville days," Uncle Guy said, standing at the mantelpiece, where he had left his cup. "Better to steal a scene than cheat the audience."

"What!" cried Aunt Nettles. "How dare you call me a cheat!"

"Terp, old boy, did you hear me call anyone a cheat?" Uncle Guy asked gaily, putting on his reading glasses. "But what I say doesn't matter a fig—it's what the score pad says."

"Cheat indeed," Aunt Nettles muttered. "Who'd need to cheat when they're playing with the likes of you?"

"Looky here—sixteen thousand two hundred and seven to sixteen thousand four hundred and ten in one game. Nettles, you amaze me! Two hundred points in one fell swoop! Or maybe your pen slipped." Uncle Guy picked up his eggnog. "There's many a slip between the cup and the lip."

"Let me see that!" Aunt Nettles cried.

"Please, Guy, put it away," Mrs. Taft pleaded. "Show a little Christmas spirit."

"He's had quite enough of my Christmas spirits already," grumbled Mr. Taft, whose good bourbon had gone into spiking the eggnog.

"And looky here," Uncle Guy went on. "Minus three hundred and two for poor Guy, in one hand. How's that possible? I've heard the moon's made of green cheese—but going down three hundred points in one hand?"

"Give me that!" Aunt Nettles screamed, leaping out of her chair.

She ran at her husband. But Uncle Guy passed the score pad off to Terpin, far more deftly than Charles could ever have passed a football.

"Let's leave it to an outside party, an impartial observer," Uncle Guy suggested. "Terp, old boy, what do you think ought to be done about this shocking score pad?"

The thick pad was like an accounting book, each of its pages covered with endless careful columns of tiny figures. They were all watching him, and as he held the pad, he felt much as he had the day he had held the ax on the Pepper Pike.

"Sometimes they team up on me, Terpin," Aunt Nettles said pitifully. "They plot against me."

"Don't tamper with the jury," said Uncle Guy. "It's up to you, Terp. What do you think would be the best thing to do about it?"

It seemed to Terpin depressing enough that he had not been invited to Melanie's party without his having to get involved in this bickering. But there was no way out now. He rose from his chair with a sigh and tossed the score pad into the fire.

For an instant everyone in the room remained silent, frozen. Then Aunt Nettles gave a shriek and fell to her knees, reaching in over the brass fender. To Terpin's surprise, his uncle and his mother shrieked as well. But the hundreds of yellow pages of figures curled and blackened in the flames before anyone could pluck them out. A tomblike silence fell over the room.

"Good Lord," Mrs. Taft said finally, staring in blank horror at the flames.

"Seven years," Uncle Guy muttered dully, "up in smoke."

Aunt Nettles could manage only a gurgling sound in her throat.

"Now that you're free of the score pad, why don't you play some other games?" Terpin suggested.

But when the last blackened page had fluttered up the chimney, the three of them—his aunt, his uncle, and his mother—turned and stared at him as if he were a murderer.

For the rest of his vacation the house was like a funeral parlor. Mrs. Beale came over in the afternoons, but although the four of them sat around the green felt table as usual, no one had enough spirit to shuffle a pack of cards, and they merely stared at one another, as if in shock. Terpin slunk around the house, feeling more like a ghost than ever. He spent a great deal of time alone in his room. One night he felt so lonely and depressed that he threw the ancient Greek coin in his wastepaper basket. But when he woke the next morning, he realized he was a sleepwalker, for he found the coin clenched tightly in his hand.

So, in spite of his new unpopularity among his classmates, he was relieved when school began again. Furthermore, the beginning of the new year was always an exciting time at school, for it was then that the topic for the Haversham Award essay was announced. One icy gray afternoon, when the overhead lights were on in the classroom and the radiators were whistling under the windows, Mr. Thrushcroft came around and perched birdlike on the front of his desk.

"As you know, class," the teacher said, looking out over them, "the importance of this essay in determining your semester grade is beyond estimation. Each of you has read a paper to the class already—but these were like trial flights. This is for the Haversham Award. I know—the very name sends thrills of expectation down your spines . . ."

And strange to say, he was not far wrong. No one was looking out the steamy windows or at the clock over the door: they all had their eyes fixed on the teacher, as if he were a general about to lead them into battle.

". . . the Haversham Award. The very name conjures up pictures of victory and glory and honored scholars from the past, whose names are engraved on the golden plaque in the hallway. Consider. Once one of your names joins theirs, once your name is added to the select list of Haversham Award winners, it will never be rubbed away! It is not unlike, if you will, the famous old poem: 'An angel writing in a book of gold . . . the names of those who love the Lord.' For that name will be etched not only on the golden plaque and announced in assembly but also etched forever in the memory of our school and our town. Consider that, class, and let that high consideration console you over the next week of struggling and striving with words, sentences, and paragraphs."

At this point Mr. Thrushcroft, rocking happily, paused to let his stirring speech sink in. Then he took a sealed envelope from his pocket.

"As you are aware, class, it rests not with me but with the principal himself to make the yearly choice of subject for the Haversham Award essays—which is as it should be. As you are also well aware, having concentrated your attention for the last few months on the ancient world, it is from that quiver that our arrow will be plucked. But what that particular arrow is—the subject which will occupy your minds so completely for the next week—not even I know yet."

Mr. Thrushcroft slit the envelope dramatically. As he pulled out and unfolded the piece of paper, rows of greedy eyes were intent on his spidery fingers.

"The topic for this year's Haversham Award Essay Competition," he read out, "is 'The Life and Death of . . . Socrates'!"

Hearing the name gave Terpin a warm feeling inside: it was like hearing the name of a friend. But the name had quite a different effect on everyone else in the room. Mr. Thrushcroft stopped beaming, while all the students turned in their places to glare into the back row at him, Terpin—all except Charles Ackley, who simply stopped drumming his supple fingers on his desk. But frown though he might, it was not for Mr. Thrushcroft to question the choice of the principal.

"Well!" was all the teacher allowed himself on that subject. "And now, class, I am going to let you out early so you can all set to work straight-away. Into the breach!"

The class charged out the door and down the hall into the library. A minute later, all nine books on Socrates owned by the school library had been checked out for the week. Those who had been too slow, too tame, or too polite to get hold of one straggled back sadly down the hall behind the parade of victors, which was composed of four proud boys and five proud girls.

Meanwhile, Terpin was left alone in the class-room with Mr. Thrushcroft, and as Terpin gathered up his books, the teacher remarked dryly:

"Well, Mr. Taft, I suppose you think you're going to get your name on the plaque?"

But Terpin only shrugged as he ambled out of the room. He collected his things from the cloakroom and strolled out into the hall. Before he reached the doors, however, he crossed the path of his classmates, returning from the library.

They grabbed him and backed him up against the glass case holding the golden Haversham Award plaque.

"Lucky stiff!" they shouted angrily.

"All you have to do is rewrite your old paper!"

"Some people get all the breaks!"

Terpin sighed, knowing they never would have treated him like this a few months ago. Then the fullback of the football team, a pimply farm-boy who already weighed 190 pounds, grabbed a hank of Terpin's hair and gave it such a playful tug that quite a bit came out by the roots. A girl gave his toes a good-natured stomp and cried, "I don't think it's fair!"

"Oh, shut your silly face," said Charles Ackley, coming to his friend's defense. "It's not his fault."

"Shut your own," the girl replied. "Who said it was? I only said it isn't fair."

"We could give him the treatment," the fullback suggested. "That way he might learn not to make his paper too slick."

This idea seemed agreeable to all concerned, and in a minute they had dragged Terpin down the back steps and out onto the snowy playing field. While several of them held him in place, others began to pack snow around him, beginning at his feet. In spite of Charles's protests they all worked industriously, and soon Terpin found himself waist deep in a huge block of snow—which was far from pleasant, for his shirt had come untucked and some of the snow had slipped under his coat against his bare back. Before long, he was encased up to his chin. Then the fullback leaned his face right up to his and leered at him.

"Say you won't make your paper too slick, Taft, and we won't go any further."

Terpin tried to turn away from the pimply face, but his neck was too well packed.

"I don't know what you're making a fuss about," he said gloomily. "I'm not even going to write on Socrates."

These words produced a momentary silence. Everyone stared at him. Then the fullback gave a snort. "Who do you think we are, to fall for that?" he asked.

"Sometimes I can't help thinking you're a

bunch of sheep," Terpin murmured, unable to lie.

"Terpin!" Charles cried. "Don't make it worse!"

But this advice came too late. Three snow-balls, in quick succession, pelted the unmoving target of his head.

"And there's more where those came from," someone observed, "if you don't come clean with us."

"Yeah, tell us the truth."

Terpin's face was now ragged with snow, but still he made the mistake of smiling as he told them he *had* "come clean," that he was telling the truth.

"That does it," the fullback muttered, hoisting a great block of snow onto his shoulder.

And had Charles not made a fist and given the block a punch, causing it to break apart, it might well have fallen squarely on Terpin's head.

"Listen to him," Charles insisted.

"All right, Terpin," said Melanie, stepping forward. "How come you're not going to write on Socrates?"

"Because I already did," he said simply.

"But you'd win the Haversham Award," came a chorus of voices.

Terpin tried to explain himself. In spite of what their eccentric history teacher had said, Terpin found it hard to believe that having one's name etched on a gold plaque was really the most wonderful thing imaginable.

"You mean that, Terpin?" Melanie asked. "Cross your heart?"

"I'd cross my heart if I could," Terpin replied.

"Sure he means it," said Charles, starting to dig his friend out.

When Charles had freed his chest and arms, Terpin crossed his heart, and then the fullback pitched in, helping dig him the rest of the way out. Terpin was set free. The others all went back into the school building for their coats. Charles came out again quickly, shaking one of his hands.

"Say, that was a close call," he said, grinning as he came up to Terpin. "There was a piece of ice in that block."

"Did you hurt your fingers?" Terpin asked, concerned.

"Nah."

Terpin smiled. "Want to come skiing?"

For a moment Charles simply stared at him. Then he leaned back and laughed.

"Haven't you had your fill of snow for one day, Terpin?"

"There's a difference," Terpin said, still smiling, "between being packed in ice like a codfish and skiing through the tamarack trees."

"Well, I suppose you're right. . . . But b-ball starts next week, and after practice I'll have to get cracking on the paper."

"Basketball . . . papers . . ." Terpin shook his head sadly. "If you won't come skiing, I wish you'd practice the piano."

"Give me one good reason I should cut b-ball."

Terpin heaved a sigh.

"Because you're worse at basketball than football, Charles. Your feet were made for tripping over. But your fingers—"

"That's a fine thing to say, when I just saved your skin!" Charles cried angrily.

"But I've said it plenty of times. You know yourself—"

"Hey, shove it, will you? Listen, Taft, I've really had it with you."

Turning his back, Charles started to plod away through the snow. Terpin called after him, explaining he had spoken not to insult him but out of true friendship, but Charles continued gymward. Once he tripped, but when he caught his balance, he just plodded faster, never looking back.

Terpin turned with a sad shrug and walked home, avoiding the Pepper Pike, where the chamber of commerce was supervising the destruction of the trees. As he moved through the icy gray afternoon, it struck him that he had now lost his last friend—for the parting look on Charles's face had been bitter indeed. He had lost even Uncle Guy: since the incident with the score pad, even his merry uncle had not had a single word to say to him. All he had left were the new friends he had made in his own mind, the image of the man in the black greatcoat and the image of the ancient Greek philosopher with the flowing white beard. One of these friends had been dead for almost two months, the other for over two thousand years. So in a way he himself was like a ghost.

And yet, unpopular and ghostlike as he was, he had a strange feeling even now that he had never been so well befriended.

# 5

Terpin also had the snowshoe hares. Like a ghost he would glide after them, up hill and down dale, his skis whistling on the snow like the runners on a sled. And the hares seemed to enjoy the sport as well, for instead of bolting off into holes they always led him a merry chase through the woods, leaving behind their miniature snowshoe prints.

One afternoon toward the end of that week a particularly playful hare led him on a longer chase than usual. Every now and then this hare would actually stop in its tracks, look back over its shoulder, and wait for him to catch up before bounding off again. The hare seemed to be playing a game

with him: it was almost as if they were communicating. But in his delight at the sport Terpin finally lost his bearings. And in its delight the hare finally lost its wariness of what lay ahead. Skiing out into a clearing, Terpin suddenly heard a splintering crash. The hare was perched ahead, looking back at him over its shoulder. As the bulldozer crashed out of a thicket, heading straight for the hare, Terpin yelled. But the dumb animal remained stubbornly frozen—secure, perhaps, in the camouflage of its white fur against the snow.

"Jump!" Terpin cried.

But the hare vanished under the heavy tread of the machine. When the bulldozer had passed on, there was a red splotch left in its tracks, and Terpin felt as if his own heart had been crushed.

The operator of the bulldozer made no response to his cries, could probably not even hear them over the engine. Terpin skied angrily around the thicket and came face to face with the chamber of commerce. Only then did he realize that the hare had led him right down to the edge of the forbidden Pepper Pike.

The ring of gentlemen in overcoats was collected as before on the roadside, but since his last visit here the scene had changed. Now the men were surveying an expanse of fallen birches, which looked like bloodless corpses on a battlefield. And as luck would have it, this afternoon seemed to be another important occasion, for the town mayor was there. Mrs. Minor, standing a little apart from the others by a block of granite, was wearing a ribbon on the lapel of her coat, and a pair of knee-high boots. She was not a large woman, but her voice was very large indeed, easily audible over the rumbling bulldozer in the distance.

". . . a day that will be fondly recollected by our grandchildren, and their grandchildren in turn," she was booming. "What's more, I don't doubt that this date will be made a permanent bank holiday."

At this the mayor paused in her speech and cast a glance at Terpin's father, who nodded vigorously. The mayor then caught sight of Terpin.

"And speaking of grandchildren," she said,

"I'm pleased to notice that we have here among us today a representative of the younger generation."

Terpin, who was standing there in a daze, leaning on his ski poles, saw all the members of the chamber of commerce turn and look at him with sudden approval.

"I'm sure it pleases our young friend here, too, to know that when the rest of us are dead and gone, he will have the honor of being the last living witness of my . . . of the Great Step Forward." The mayor smiled cordially. "It pleases you, my young friend, to think of that?"

"To think that you'll be dead and gone, ma'am?" Terpin asked in confusion, staring at the round, beribboned woman. "Or that I'll be the last living witness?"

"The wit of a future politician!" she said with delight. "Perhaps you'll hold public office one day, perhaps you'll rise as high as deputy mayor—who knows, perhaps even mayor!"

(Yes, even now, as the train was carrying him back to North Haven for the first time in over thirty years, even now, holding as he did a public office somewhat higher than the mayorship of a little town, he remembered those words perfectly.)

"But you must admit, my young friend," the mayor went on, "it's an affecting experience, being here today."

Terpin glanced around at the corpses of the trees and admitted it was an affecting experience.

"And really, it's not for us but for the likes of our young friend here that we're laying this cornerstone today," she went on, placing a gloved hand on the block of granite. "You must be proud."

Mr. Taft came over and nudged his son out toward the great lady. But Terpin—who could not understand why these adults, who seemed so happy with their project, were always saying they were doing everything for his generation—squinted his face into a pained expression.

"Not proud?" Mrs. Minor said.

He shook his head.

"If not proud, my young friend, then how do you feel?"

"I feel sort of sick," he admitted.

"Sick, did you say?"

"Yes, ma'am."

"Sick, did he say?"

"Impossible," murmured numerous voices.

"I didn't think he said that," she agreed, nodding. "You didn't say sick, did you?"

"You shouldn't have cut down the trees," Terpin murmured.

"Ah, I see," said the mayor. "But if we hadn't cut down the trees, we could hardly have started to build, could we now? Anyway, there are hundreds of trees left across the pike."

"But it isn't the same," Terpin said. "People used to like to drive into North Haven because all the white trees made it like a dream. But this doesn't seem like North Haven anymore."

He stared out across the log-littered snow toward the thicket, beyond which the broken hare was lying in its frozen grave.

"It's all my fault," he muttered. "If I hadn't chased him, he wouldn't have come down here."

"What's that now?" the mayor asked.

Terpin looked up. "Nothing," he muttered.

Suddenly he got a box on the side of his head.

"How dare you be short with the mayoress!" his father cried. "Get home this minute, and I'll deal with you later."

But just then the bulldozer came crashing back over the thicket, and instead of obeying his father, Terpin merely stared at the horrible machine, which had felled the hare and so many birches. Mr. Taft, excusing himself from his fellow members of the chamber of commerce, grabbed Terpin by the collar and told him to undo his bindings.

Their walk home was not talkative, although Mr. Taft did mutter something about military academies. When they entered the large white clapboard house with green shutters, Mr. Taft advised Terpin to go up to his room and think over his disrespectful behavior. But then a voice called out from the card room:

"Is that you, dear? Aren't you early?"

It was Mrs. Taft; yet the voice was plaintive and flat, with none of its old sweetness. Mr. Taft led Terpin into the card room, where the four regular players were sitting at their usual places around the felt-topped table. But there was no fire in the grate, nor were there any cards in their hands. A strand of Aunt Nettles's iron-colored hair had come loose from her usually tight snood, and the ice had melted in Uncle Guy's glass. They were all staring blankly at each other, like zombies.

"I thought you people played canasta this time of day," said Mr. Taft, who was more or less oblivious of household events.

He was answered by a long silence. He repeated his observation, and finally Uncle Guy seemed to focus on him.

"Not since Terpin burnt the score," Uncle Guy said dully. "Seven years of our lives."

"Nearly eight, actually," sighed Mrs. Beale, the next-door neighbor.

"Nearly eight, actually," said Uncle Guy like an empty echo. "And so, you see, we'd have to start from scratch."

"Start from scratch," Aunt Nettles said.

"Why'd you do that, anyway, Terpin?" Mr. Taft asked.

"Why, indeed," said Uncle Guy, staring at his

diluted drink. "He might as well have opened our veins."

"Opened our veins," echoed Aunt Nettles.

"But why?"

"He said something about how we oughtn't always do the same thing," Uncle Guy replied, as if Terpin were not in the room, were invisible.

"Oughtn't do the same thing!" cried Mr. Taft. "And just now he was telling us we ought to have left it the same! The Pepper Pike, I mean. What's the matter with you, boy?"

The reproachful looks on all their faces, even his mother's, gave Terpin a pang. Touching the rough old Greek coin in his pocket, he murmured that he had only done what he thought to be right and true.

"Right and true?" grumbled Mr. Taft. "Talking back to the mayoress? I only hope they can straighten you out in a military academy, because that's where you're going."

The faces of the cardless players turned to him.

"Amen," they said all together.

Terpin looked at them in dismay. He had never really cared for smashing people in football; a military academy would surely be even worse.

"But you don't understand," he said. "The bulldozer killed a hare."

At this, a little of the red actually seemed to drain out of his father's face.

"Oh, I see," said Mr. Taft, who was not really a tyrant. "That's why you were acting so strangely?"

Terpin nodded.

"All right, son," Mr. Taft sighed. "I'm going to give you one more chance. But just one more—then off you go."

# 6

Outside the tall classroom windows the limbs of the bare elm creaked in the wind, while inside the room the radiators gave off faint toots of steam, like a train in the distance. Mr. Thrushcroft was perched on the front of his desk between a stack of essays and a pile of brown envelopes. As he addressed the class, he kept his frail arms tucked at his sides, with his fingers laced over his belly.

"Ten days ago, class," he said, "I gave you an assignment of singular moment and importance. I instructed you to begin your Haversham essays."

Unlacing his fingers, he set one of his spidery hands atop the stack of essays.

"And here they are, completed and graded—signed, sealed, and delivered, if you will. I've no need to reiterate how critical these essays are to your report cards."

And he set his other spidery hand atop the pile of brown envelopes.

"I think I can say in all conscience that the general quality of these essays was better than fair. Some, of course, were superior to others. Others, naturally, were inferior to some. But on the whole—quite pleasing."

Mr. Thrushcroft beamed, uniting his hands once more.

"Needless to say, one of these essays is destined to earn its author a touch of immortality, a wreath of laurel, as it were. One of you shall, as the poet said, 'dwell on the heights of mankind.' But just who this person shall be—that is not for me to decide. The principal has read over those essays which I picked out as the cream of the crop, and he will render his decision in assembly tomorrow. This is as it should be. So much, however, I shall tell you: of those I gave him, three essays were from members of this class—Danny Schwartz, Holly Patch, and Melanie Minor."

As he paused for effect, a moan rose up from the class, as if from the site of a massacre. Such was the prestige of the Haversham Award that nearly everyone contributed to the woeful noise—although, of course, the three students just named were grinning at one another like members of a new secret club. Mr. Thrushcroft smiled his general sympathy.

"There, there, there," he said. "It's only right that you should be bitterly disappointed. You must remember, however, that we cannot all win the award—we cannot all bear the palm. Otherwise, the award would quite lose its meaning, wouldn't it? Look at it in this light. Although it's natural for each of you to regret not being first, a certain pride should also be taken in not being last. Of course, the glory of firsthood is the great goal in all that we do; but remember, it's also an accomplishment of sorts to escape lasthood. For to be last is to be covered with the ignominious rag of shame."

The woeful noises ceased. Anxious looks began to appear on faces all over the room. Was it possible that Mr. Thrushcroft, peculiar as he was, intended to do such an unheard-of thing as name the writer of the worst paper?

"To be last!" the teacher said balefully. "What a dread circumstance that is, class. And just as one must always be first among you, another, by the same token, must always be last. But have no fear—you won't all have to spend a sleepless night. You need not wait for any assembly tomorrow to know where that awful lot has fallen. For although the principal chooses the finest essay, it's my prerogative to choose the poorest."

Palms had begun to sweat all over the room. Unfair as it seemed, they were being marched into another battle. Mr. Thrushcroft prolonged the moment of tension by taking out a handkerchief, blowing his beakish nose, and murmuring something about the weather.

"It was," he said finally, "a simple enough choice. For one of you conceived the unfortunate idea of not writing on the assigned subject at all.

One among you had the poor judgment to leave Socrates, as it were, in the lurch."

As if a cease-fire had been declared, a great sigh of relief swept down the columns of seated students, safe in the knowledge that they had at least written on Socrates. Mr. Thrushcroft pulled one of the essays from the stack at his side.

"We have here, class, an essay entitled not 'The Life and Death of Socrates' or 'The Teachings of Socrates.' No. Believe it or not, this particular essay is entitled 'The Coins of Ancient Greece.'"

A few snickers were heard around the classroom. Then, one by one, smiling faces turned around to look into the back row, and Terpin could not help shifting uncomfortably in his chair.

"I wonder, Mr. Taft," the teacher went on pleasantly, "if you would be good enough to tell us why you failed to write on the topic assigned?"

"I already wrote on Socrates, sir," Terpin said.

"Oh, I see. And what kept you from writing on him again?"

"I could have rewritten my old paper—but I

thought it would be better to write on something new. The coins are very interesting. Did you know that the owl was a symbol of wisdom?" He took his ancient coin out of his pocket. "Look, I have—"

"*You* thought it would be better to write on something new," Mr. Thrushcroft interrupted him cuttingly. "And just who do you think you are to make a decision like that?"

Now everyone in the room, even Charles Ackley, was looking around at him, snickering. It really was too much for him to take, so Terpin looked down, settling his eyes on the seated, bearded man on the front of his coin. In answer to the teacher's question, he could only mumble his name, Terpin Taft.

"So you're Terpin Taft, are you?" Mr. Thrushcroft said, lifting one of the brown envelopes from the pile at his side. "Well, I'll tell you something, young man—when your father sees your report card, you might very well wish you were someone else . . . might very well wish you were far away from North Haven—

as, for that matter, I'm sure you do now, to hide your humiliation from the eyes of your friends."

But although Terpin felt sad, he was not, he realized, ashamed.

"But I don't feel humiliated," he said, lifting his eyes. He looked from the teacher to Melanie to Charles. "Anyway, I don't think they're my friends."

"They're not?" said Mr. Thrushcroft. "Well, I must say, that doesn't surprise me."

The bell rang. But for once the class did not stampede out into the cloakroom. They stayed at their desks and watched Terpin pocket his coin and collect his things, watched him with a strange mixture of horror, pity, and curiosity on their faces. Terpin, feeling a little troubled, walked up to Charles's desk in the front row.

"Maybe I wasn't telling the truth," Terpin said. "Maybe you're still my friend, Charles. Do you have any money?"

Charles stared at him, aghast. "A few bucks," he muttered. "I got to buy some shoes for b-ball."

"May I have it?" Terpin asked.

"My money? Are you crazy?"

Terpin shrugged, then he turned and walked out of the room.

He strolled out under the bare elm in front of school, where he used to meet Melanie after practice, and glanced across the town green at the snow-capped statue of the Union soldier. A shudder went through him at the thought of a military academy, which would surely be his fate once his report card reached home. He trudged out of North Haven to the train station and sat on a bench on the platform in the icy wind. Glancing sadly over his shoulder, he took what he supposed would be his last look at North Haven. Why should he ever come back?

The southbound train pulled in. He had no money for a ticket, had only his old Greek coin. But, as it turned out, a kindly conductor named George let him ride for free.

# 7

And now, over thirty years later, the kindly conductor was an old man with a flowing white beard, and Terpin was again riding for free—not because he had no money, but because the train line categorically refused to take any of it, considering it such a high honor to have him on board. When he had written out his autograph for the conductor, several passengers worked up the nerve to ask him for the same—although one lawyer was content merely "to shake the hand of the youngest Chief Justice of the Supreme Court in our nation's history."

As it happened, there was also a battalion of reporters on the train, who had been lying in wait for him to awaken from his nap. This group of men and women wanted neither autographs nor handshakes but interviews. At first, as they crowded the aisle by his seat, Terpin shook his head. Over the years he had often been disappointed by "interviews," for he had seen that when they appeared in print, the truth of the matter was often sacrificed to some ulterior purpose of the reporter's. But as he surveyed this group of reporters, he noticed that one of them, a middle-aged man in a snap-brim hat, bore a remarkable resemblance to him.

"Well, I'm sure I don't have anything very enlightening to say," Terpin murmured, "but I suppose I could give an interview. Only to one of you, though—I can't answer more than a question at a time."

Terpin pointed to the reporter who looked like him. As the others dispersed, grumbling, Terpin asked the delighted reporter if, in return for an interview, the man would be kind enough to do him a small favor.

"A favor?" the reporter said, doffing his hat

respectfully as he sat down in the empty seat beside him. "Why, Your Honor, it would be an . . . an honor."

The man took out his notepad and began the interview.

"How'd you ever manage to get to the top of the Supreme Court, sir?" he asked. "Is it true you started out as a bellhop without a penny to your name?"

Terpin smiled vaguely. "That's true—although I was lucky enough to have something better than a penny."

"Something better than a penny," the reporter murmured, jotting this down. "And then you went to night school, studied law?"

"That's right."

"No help from your family or old friends?"

"I haven't seen my family or my old friends in over thirty years."

The reporter duly noted this.

"You ever hear from them, Your Honor?"

Yes, Terpin had heard from them—more and more frequently, in fact, as the years had gone by.

The first letters to find him had been from his mother. These letters had described how the four canasta players had taken to Parcheesi—and then, with mounting enthusiasm, to cribbage, bridge, and quadruple solitaire, until finally they had a different game for every day of the week. They had quit keeping running scores, so resentments no longer built up, and his mother had mentioned that Aunt Nettles had grown a little pleasanter and that the excitement of having something different each day had actually diminished Uncle Guy's drinking. In latter years Terpin had also begun to receive rather sad letters from Charles Ackley. Charles had become a concert pianist, but he had not attained the first rank, which he blamed on his lack of diligence in his early days. When Terpin became famous, he had received an elaborate and flattering invitation from Mr. Thrushcroft to give an address to the school on the historic subject of his choice; but having been denied such a choice in the past, Terpin had decided it was only right to refuse the honor now. About ten years ago he had also begun to hear from

Melanie Minor, who had married and divorced and finally, on her mother's death, become mayor of North Haven: she had wanted him to use his influence to get her invited to a mayors' conference in the nation's capital. But North Haven was far too small a town to qualify her for such an honor, and he had refused to lie about the town's population to the National Council of Mayors. The fact was, North Haven had even fewer citizens now than in his boyhood. For in the end the Heavenly Havens scheme had failed miserably: the ticky-tack cluster of cabins and chalets had turned the once-quaint town into the laughingstock of the county, and tourists had studiously avoided it. And so it was that Terpin had never, in all those years, heard from his father. The North Haven Savings and Loan had still not been robbed, but for the bank, which had financed the "Great Step Forward," the failure of the project had been more disastrous than any robbery. Against robberies the bank held insurance, but not against poor investments. In the end Mr. Taft, utterly ruined, had suffered a heart attack and then an apoplectic stroke, which left the poor man bedridden, his face permanently scarlet. For the past dozen years Terpin had been paying the bills of the nursing home where his father was cared for, as well as sending another weekly check to support his aging mother and aunt and uncle.

"So you got where you are today without the help of family or friends?" the newspaperman went on.

"Oh, I'd never have gotten anywhere without the help of my friends," Terpin said. "Only they were dead."

"Dead friends," the journalist said, noting this down.

"But alive to me."

"But alive to you," the journalist murmured, writing. "That's pretty interesting, Your Honor—juicy stuff. But still, it must be a thrill, returning home in such glory after all these years."

As for this, Terpin was not at all sure. How could he have refused their invitation when they said they were changing the name of the town to

North Tafton? And furthermore, he had long ago put aside his bitterness over the way they had virtually driven him out of town, and he did long to lay eyes on his mother and aunt and uncle and father again before they died. And yet, as the train neared North Haven, or North Tafton, he was beginning to have second thoughts.

"You mentioned something about a favor, Your Honor," the reporter said, closing up his notepad. "Just name it."

"Well, sir, do you notice something about us?" Terpin asked.

"You mean how I'm pretty near a dead ringer for you? Yeah, sure, I've had plenty of people come up and ask me for my autograph—or your autograph, I should say. It's kind of fun." He laughed, fingering the lapel of his rather soiled trench coat. "Of course, not when I'm in this old thing."

Terpin glanced at his own fine chesterfield overcoat.

"Would you trade with me?" Terpin asked.

# 8

Wearing the soiled trench coat and the snap-brim hat pulled down over his eyes, Terpin walked to the back of the train and got off at North Haven from the very last car. Up in the middle of the platform, the school band was playing, and a delegation of leading citizens was there to greet the reporter, who was wearing Terpin's fine chesterfield coat. As Terpin ambled toward the crowd, he recognized Melanie Minor, plump and wearing knee-high boots as her mother had, her harvest-moon hair now gray, at the head of the welcoming committee. This committee seemed to be composed mostly of the chamber of commerce, but there were a few snowy heads in the delegation, and tears of joy and sorrow filled his eyes to see the ancient versions of his mother and aunt and uncle.

The welcoming committee did not linger on the platform, for it was only the beginning of March and there was a gusty wind. The mayor guided the reporter down the steps into a waiting car. The others—including the band, playing a military march—followed in a parade. Terpin joined the stragglers behind the band. Soon they reached the town green, where the rest of North Haven was gathered, most of them seated in bleachers borrowed from the school for the occasion. A little stage had been erected just behind the statue of the Union soldier, beside which there now stood another statue hidden by a huge tarpaulin. Although the green was rather muddy, the lead car drove right up onto it, leaving tread marks. The mayor led the reporter and the most influential citizens onto the stage, over which there was stretched a banner reading: WELCOME TO NORTH TAFTON.

Terpin found a seat in the bleachers just behind the three ancient members of his family. During the mayoral address, his mother's hat blew off, and he was able to retrieve it for her.

"You mustn't catch cold, madam," he said, his eyes smiling from under his snap-brim hat as he handed hers back.

"Oh, I'm far too happy and proud to catch cold this afternoon," his mother said, thanking him with a quick smile and then turning her attention back to the stage.

The mayoral address boomed out over the loudspeakers. At the end of it, the mayor gave a signal, and a pair of workmen came forward out of the crowd and pulled the tarpaulin off the new statue. As the bronze figure of Terpin in his Supreme Court robes was unveiled, the entire town applauded.

When the applause finally died down, the mayor turned to the reporter, seated behind her on the stage, and said coyly: "Now I'll be able to see my old beau every day. What do you think of it, Your Honor?"

"Why, it's very nice—very nice, indeed!" replied the reporter, who was clearly enjoying having these honors heaped on him.

His response set off another wave of applause,

and Terpin, who was relieved to be in the audience, joined in the clapping. Over the years he had learned many such tricks as this, for although his penchant for the truth held him in good stead in his judge's chambers, it had often led to trouble in everyday life. The truth, he had learned, was an unwelcome guest. It was obnoxious, ill-mannered; no one much cared for its company. Which accounted, Terpin sometimes thought, for why he had always remained more or less alone, why people often detected "something lonely about his face." Had he been sitting on the stage at this moment, for example, he would have been forced to reply to the mayor's question by saying, "Why, the statue looks perfectly ridiculous there. You have the whole green to work with, and you put the one statue right next to the other. It's like taking a photograph with your subjects crammed into one corner." Really, it was just as well that he was in the audience. And besides, it made no difference to anyone whether he was really onstage or not, for of course they had not come to see him, Terpin Taft, but a figure, the Chief Justice.

"Good old Terp," he heard Uncle Guy say to Aunt Nettles, nudging her in a strangely affectionate way. "He's gone gray, but I'd know him anywhere."

After the addresses by the mayor and the deputy mayor, a wizened old man, who looked rather like a stork with a cane, hopped and hobbled across the stage to the microphone. It was none other than Mr. Thrushcroft, long retired perhaps, but as long-winded as ever. Much to Terpin's amusement, the birdlike man dwelled on the "fond memories" he cherished of a "bright boy with a mop of hair," who he had "always suspected would do great things."

"I recall in particular a paper he once gave my class on the subject of the ancient Greek philosopher Aristotle. Do you still retain a love for Aristotle?" he asked, turning to the reporter seated behind him.

"Indeed I do!" the reporter replied, saving Terpin from the unpleasant duty of having to correct the old teacher, who seemed to have grown senile.

"Aristotle!" Mr. Thrushcroft said with a sigh of

pleasure. "What a fund of knowledge was there! Surely your thorough study of Aristotelian thought has been the basis of your meteoric rise, the fieldstone foundation, if you will, of the towering edifice of your career?"

"Without a doubt!" the reporter replied.

"Aristotle! Surely 'the noblest Roman of them all,' as the poet said," the senile history teacher went on. "Just as you yourself are surely one of the noblest citizens of our own age . . ."

The speech rambled on in this vein for a quarter of an hour, making reference to the "glory of firsthood" and giving everyone to understand that his early encouragement was almost single-handedly responsible for Terpin's later accomplishments. No doubt the man actually believed this to be true; but Terpin could see in the opposite bleacher that many of the band members, who could not wear mittens and whose uniforms had no pockets, were suffering in the cold. Finally Mr. Thrushcroft was led off the stage, although not before he had turned and planted a fond kiss on the reporter's half-frozen cheek.

Even then the gathering could not adjourn to the Town Building at the end of the green, where the luncheon-reception was to be held. There was another speaker to be introduced.

"And now we shall hear from a member of the school's graduating class," the mayor said, "who will welcome the Honorable Terpin Taft in the name of the young people of our fine community. I give you Sean Hoolihan, who is not only this year's valedictorian and Haversham Award winner but captain of both the football team and the ski team as well."

Terpin heard this with interest, for a ski team had not existed in his day. A young man with a freckled face and moppish hair, not unlike his own in his schooldays, walked nervously across the stage and proceeded to clear his throat several times, which over the microphone produced a sound like cracking walnuts. This embarrassing noise seemed to add to the poor fellow's nervousness. To make matters worse, a strong wind suddenly sprang up, carrying tiny flakes of snow, and his speech, written out on a piece of paper, began to flutter in his hand. When he finally managed to read the first sentence, he could not keep his trembling voice from rising into a squeak.

"Without any question . . . this is the proudest . . . the proudest moment of my life." Each time his voice cracked, Sean Hoolihan had to break off, for the high-pitched sound made the loudspeakers hum and squeal. The poor fellow turned beet red. "The proudest and happiest moment of my life," he went on bravely, "to have the honor of welcoming . . . the first citizen of North Tafton back home." At this moment he turned to the reporter, as no doubt his speech instructed him to. "Little did I ever . . . ever dream that I would be standing on a . . . on a stage with the Chief Justice of the Supreme Court. Little did I—"

Suddenly a fierce gust of wind and snow swept across the green. It rattled the makeshift stage and ripped the banner over it. The speech flew out of Sean's hand, and he barely caught up with it before it fluttered into the audience. The mayor came forward to the microphone with a smile. "It seems it's still winter," she said. "Perhaps we had better hear the rest of Sean's speech inside."

The dignitaries filed off the shaky stage, while the audience clambered down out of the bleachers. The muddy green was quickly turning white, and the crowd followed the mayor and the reporter through the snow toward the Town Building. Following their teachers' orders, the young people hung back to let their elders get in out of the weather first, and Terpin hung back, too, falling into step beside Sean Hoolihan.

"Good snow," Terpin remarked. "Nice and dry."

"Yeah," Sean agreed, looking enthusiastically toward the hills.

"Go get your skis, why don't you?" Terpin suggested.

Sean gave him a suspicious sidelong glance. "Now? What, are you nuts?"

Terpin smiled, stopping below the steps to the Town Building.

"Well, it's probably the last snow of the season."

Sean paused, too, stuffing his hands in his coat pockets.

"You a reporter or something?" he asked, looking

at the press card stuck in Terpin's hatband.

Terpin shook his head. Out of the corner of his eye he caught sight of a tall, spindly, middle-aged man watching them from the steps.

"I just thought it was a shame you should have to miss all this powder, seeing as you're a skier."

Sean looked a little longingly at the dry flakes collecting on his coat sleeve. "But I've got to give this speech, mister. It's the Chief Justice in there."

Terpin laughed, his breath turning to vapor in the snowy air.

"You mean about how this is the happiest moment of your life and all that?"

Sean stared off at the hills.

"You'd be happier up there, wouldn't you?" Terpin asked.

It was Sean's turn to laugh.

"You want me just to cut out?"

"Why not?"

"Why not? Because I'd be in the soup with everybody!"

Terpin smiled. "If you like to ski cross-country, you could come with me—though I may be kind of creaky. Or if you like downhill, you could head up there."

Sean laughed again.

"If you don't mind me saying so, mister, you've got a screw loose," he said, eyeing the soiled trench coat. "Go skiing with you when I should be in there meeting Chief Justice Taft!"

"What do you care about a Chief Justice?" Terpin asked. "Anyway, giving that speech was sheer torture for you."

"But it's an honor."

"It'd be an honor to ski with him, Sean," said the tall, spindly man on the steps.

Sean looked around. "Pardon me, Mr. Ackley?"

Terpin, too, glanced up at the man again, in whom he suddenly recognized his old friend Charles Ackley. To his surprise, Charles slipped him a wink.

"You could do a lot worse than listen to this fellow, Sean," Charles said. "And as for your speech, I can promise you the Honorable Mr. Taft won't miss it. You don't want to give it anyway, do you?"

Sean again looked off at the white hills. But

nen he took his hands out of his coat pockets and brushed the snow off his hair.

"I better go in," he said a little wistfully.

Terpin reached under his trench coat and pulled something from his pants pocket. As Sean turned to go, Terpin slipped it into the pocket of the young man's coat. When Sean had gone into the Town Building, Charles came down the steps and held out his hand. Charles's face had grown sad and a little wrinkled over the years, but as Terpin shook his hand, he noticed his fingers were still long and supple.

"No football practice today," Charles said wryly. "Would you like to come over to my house for a cup of coffee?"

Terpin smiled. "What do you say I come by in a couple hours, Charles? We could catch up a little, then maybe you could take me by this nursing home so I could see my father."

"With pleasure, Your Honor," Charles said.

"Terpin."

"With pleasure, Terpin."

For in North Tafton the winter days, like life

itself, were brief: to waste one seemed rather tragic. So Terpin walked off alone through the falling snow, recrossing the green and starting down the Pepper Pike toward the old white clapboard house with green shutters he had once called home. At his back he heard a muffled eruption of applause—for him, no doubt. A shiver of loneliness went through him, but he shook it off. He continued along and came upon a gateway with the words HEAV NLY H VENS over it. Within the gate were ticky-tack cabins and chalets that had fallen into disrepair, and everywhere around them birch trees were growing up. The snowfall was becoming heavier. Would he still be able to fit into his old boots and bindings, he wondered. Would there still be snowshoe hares nibbling the bark of the hemlocks, waiting to make his heart leap as they leapt off through the snow? Back in the distance there was another muffled roar of applause, but Terpin hardly heard it, wondering only if, after all these years, he would be able to find the secret slope that looked like the flowing white beard of Socrates.